First American Edition 2017
Kane Miller, A Division of EDC Publishing

Text copyright © Sally Rippin 2016
Illustrations copyright © Alisa Coburn 2016
Logo and design copyright © Hardie Grant Egmont 2016

First published in Australia in 2016 by Hardie Grant Egmont

For information contact:
Kane Miller, A Division of EDC Publishing
P.O. Box 470663
Tulsa, OK 74147-0663

www.kanemiller.com
www.edcpub.com
www.usbornebooksandmore.com

Library of Congress Control Number: 2016955629

Printed and bound in China
1 2 3 4 5 6 7 8 9 10

ISBN: 978-1-61067-607-6

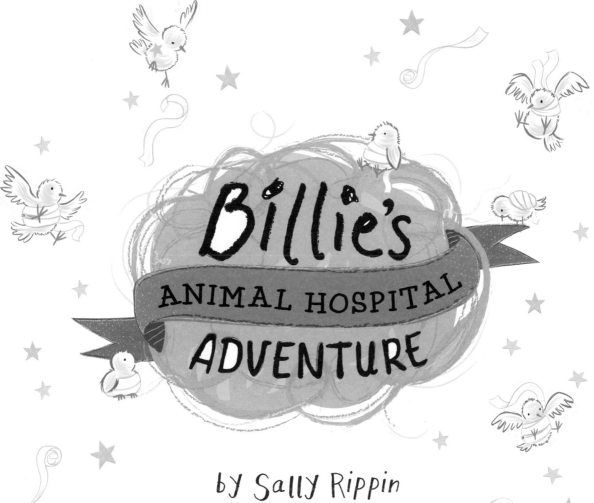

Billie's ANIMAL HOSPITAL ADVENTURE

by Sally Rippin

illustrated by Alisa Coburn

Kane Miller
A DIVISION OF EDC PUBLISHING

Billie B. Brown LIMPS into preschool.

HOP

HOP

She tripped yesterday, and now
she has a scrape on her knee.

"Look, Mr. Simon!" she says.

"Oh, that must hurt,"
Mr. Simon says.
"Look, Teddy has a hurt, too."

Poor Teddy! Billie says. Let's take him to the hospital.

Her friend Jack is ready with the ambulance. They pop Teddy in the back ...

Whir-er!
Whir-er!

... and set off with
their lights flashing.

The hospital is so busy today!

"Doctor Billie, thank goodness you're here," says Nurse Tara. "We have an emergency!"

Yip!

Yip!

Yip!

Thank you!

Some baby chicks have fallen out of their nest!
Doctor Billie examines them.

Nurse Jack dashes to the
hospital cupboard.

Billie makes the baby birds all better.

Then she gives them each a star for being so brave.

"Now, let's go fix up Teddy," Nurse Jack says to Doctor Billie.

But before they can do that …

Whir-er! Whir-er!

… another ambulance arrives.

Madame Hippo is **groaning** and *moaning, tossing* and *turning.* She ate too much ice cream!

We need medicine!

Doctor Billie says.

Nurse Jack brings a bottle of tummy medicine.

Doctor Billie gives Madame Hippo a spoonful and a star for being brave.

Then she puts a bandage on
Madame Hippo's foot to remind
her not to eat so much next time.

Madame Hippo is **very** grateful.

PHEW! It's time for a cookie and a break.
But have they forgotten someone?

Teddy!

Teddy is still in the waiting room.

Nurse Jack holds Teddy while Doctor Billie fixes up his ear.

When it's all done, Billie sticks a star on Teddy's paw for being so brave.

Thank you, Doctor Billie, he says.

Suddenly, Nurse Jack's
eyes grow wide.

"What's wrong?"
Doctor Billie asks.

He points at her knee.
Her bandage has come off!

We need more
bandages!
cries Doctor Billie.

The cupboard
is empty.

Doctor Billie's bottom lip begins to tremble.
She wants her mommy *right now!*

But her mommy is at work. What should Billie do?

Just then, Billie has an idea.

A *Super-duper* idea!

I can MAKE a bandage, she says.

She carefully tears out a square of tissue …

… and sticks it over her sore knee with some star stickers.

Now that Billie can't see the scrape, it doesn't hurt anymore.

Perfect!

Nurse Jack puts the last star on Billie's hand for being so clever and so brave.

"I think I'm finished being a doctor now," Billie says.

So she and Jack and Teddy say good-bye to everyone at the hospital.

Then they get back in the ambulance and zoom off …

Whir—er!
Whir—er!

... all the way
back to preschool.

Just in time for fruit snack.